LEAVING
JACKSONVILLE

Valerie D. Wade

I dedicate this book to the estimated six million black people that moved from the American South to the Northern, Midwestern, and Western states in search of better life.

All night long, Little Charles tossed and turned. His blue bedspread pulled away from the bed's corner and encircled his ankles. Although it was still dark, he could hear birds chirping in the distance. The house was quiet, but he couldn't contain his excitement this first Sunday morning. The older boys at church joked about what would happen when he was baptized in the St. Johns River. They warned him that alligators were lurking beneath the surface. He wasn't sure if he believed them, but he was still nervous.

Little Charles knocked on each family member's door to wake them. He wanted to ensure Papa Joe was there. Papa Joe lived in the rear of the house. He knocked lightly on the worn door, listening for Papa Joe's raspy voice.

"Who is it?"

"Papa Joe! It's first Sunday; I'm getting baptized today. Are you coming?"

1

"Yes, boy, quit yo tapping. I'm getting up. Wouldn't miss it for the world. It's 'bout time you git baptized."

"Okay, Papa Joe. I'm gonna wake everybody up." He raced around the house.

A sleepy cousin, Ivy Lee, overhearing their conversation, peeked through the cracked door. She whispered to Little Charles, "We're up and getting ready."

Little Charles hurried to the back porch, smiling widely. He sat on the first step and carried a wrinkled brown paper bag. The bag contained a small tin of Kiwi shoe polish and an old handkerchief that Papa Joe gave him. Papa Joe told him to polish his shoes every Sunday. He pulled out the black polish-stained rag saturated with the potent scent of oily polish and turned the metal lever on the side of the can to open the tin lid. He wrapped his fingers in the cloth, dabbing lightly around the inside of the well-used wax can, which revealed the shiny bottom. Patting the polish on his worn leather shoes, Little Charles carefully smoothed them evenly, as Papa Joe taught him. He used an old flattened brush to polish each shoe. Little Charles couldn't wait to show Papa Joe the shine on his shoes, which his mother, Ida Mae, found at a secondhand store. After he finished, he listened for any movement from his parent's room and raced to their door.

"Mama, wake up, wake up! We're gonna be late!"

"Lil Charles, go back to bed. It's too early! We go to church every Sunday. Be quiet before you wake your daddy."

"But Mama, it's the first Sunday! I'm getting baptized today!"

"Oh, baby, I nearly forgot. I'm getting up. Joe! Joe! Lil Charles is getting baptized this morning, and we can't be late." Ida Mae and Big

Joe had been married for 15 years, and she knew how hard it was to wake him. Their impending move, and extra guests, Cousin Ivy Lee and Willie, preoccupied her mind. They made her forget about Little Charles' baptism.

"I'm getting up. Don't worry, we won't be late," Big Joe slowly threw back the blanket, steadying his muscular six-foot frame with his large hand, using the bedpost for support. At sunrise, Big Joe sat on the porch in Papa Joe's old rocking chair. Willie sat on the first step while Papa Joe cleaned the car's hood.

The humid Florida air greeted Ida Mae at the door signaling a hot day in church, but this was Little Charles' day, and they were excited for him. Ida Mae and Big Joe wanted him baptized in their home church before they left Jacksonville. She was going to see if Ivy Lee would sing during morning service and was excited to hear her cousin's beautiful singing voice again. She bragged to all her church friends about Ivy Lee's singing. Ida Mae let him stay out a little later to spend more time with Hattie, his childhood friend since birth. Ida Mae avoided thinking about Esterline, her best friend. They had been through everything from puberty through childbirth. She was already missing her.

Ida Mae, Big Joe, Little Charles, Ivy Lee, and Willie were ready and piled into Papa Joe's old gray sedan. Little Charles got to sit in the front seat between Papa Joe and Ida Mae. Big Joe, Ivy Lee, and Willie were in the back seat. Little Charles was proud of his simple white shirt, black pants, and the tie Big Joe gave him for his special day. His tight coiled hair was neatly combed and parted on the side. His deep mocha skin accentuated his straight white teeth.

Greater Mt. Zion Baptist Church was located off a dirt road near the wide mouth of the St. Johns River. A line of hurried parishioners filed into the tiny white church with the peeling paint and patched-up stained glass windows. Many women wore enormous hats and carried fans for the long first Sunday service. Ida Mae wore her favorite straw hat and began fanning herself in the stifling heat on the ride over.

They walked towards the right side of the church. Ivy Lee headed to the choir stand while Little Charles joined three other baptism candidates. One was Little Charles' age, one was a teen girl, and one was a younger boy. The youngest candidate had a serious demeanor and large brown eyes. In the middle, two boys were making faces at the female candidate. The eldest and most immature of the three was a medium brown-skinned boy with sandy brown curly hair, chubby with deep-set dimples. His white shirt's buttons strained against his protruding stomach. The only female candidate sat upright, her hands clasped tightly in her lap and her legs crossed at the ankles, her thick wavy hair freshly platted against her caramel skin.

Ida Mae watched as Papa Joe moved to the front of the chapel with the other deacons to begin the devotional prayer. She kept looking over at Little Charles to make sure he was quiet. She knew one glance from Papa Joe would settle him down.

The time had come in the service to collect tithes and offerings. Big Joe, a trustee, headed to the rear of the church to pass around the wicker collection baskets. The entire family was looking forward to the baptism that would take place after the service. They knew the first Sunday was sacred and waited patiently until communion was served.

7

Ida Mae stood before the pulpit with the Mother's Board to help remove the white sheet covering this Sunday's communion. She thought about how much she was going to miss her home church. Big Joe and Ida Mae grew up in this church and were married there. Aunt Lillian told them all about her Baptist church in Detroit and was eager for them to join. She told Ivy Lee the choir could use her help.

Ida Mae reminisced on the memories of many family members they had lost over the years. She still imagined Big Mama sitting at the end of the pew in the second row. Papa Joe and the other deacons passed around the silver tray with the small white crackers, followed by the silver container with the tiny glasses of grape juice. When he got to Little Charles' row, he noticed Little Charles and the other boy his age shuffling around in the pew, and he gave Little

Charles an intense glare to let him know it was not a time to be acting up.

All the congregation was on their feet after Ivy Lee's rendition of *Amazing Grace*. When the service ended, Reverend Williams announced the names of the baptism candidates as they stood one by one. He also summoned Ida Mae, Big Joe, and Papa Joe to the front to thank them for their service and to bless them with their approaching relocation. They all teared up. Little Charles displayed a nervous smile as his family and the congregation filed out of the church.

The teenage girl wore all white, including a white head covering, and all three boys wore white T-shirts and dark-colored pants. Ida Mae helped them into their white robes to cover their clothing. They followed Reverend Williams in a procession around the church's rear. They walked down the gravel path to the sidewalk in the grassy area. Reverend Williams and one deacon waded from the shore until the water was waist-high. The parishioners gathered closer and began singing the familiar chorus of the baptismal hymnal, *Take Me to the Water.*

"Take me to the waaah-ter, take me to the waah-ter, take me to the water, to be baptized." As each candidate apprehensively entered the murky water, Little Charles signaled to the minister he wanted to be first, and Reverend Williams obliged.

Little Charles' eyes widened as the Reverend placed his hand over his face and immersed him in the river while reciting, "I baptize you in the name of The Father, the Son, and the Holy Ghost."

Little Charles grinned when he emerged from the water. With tears streaming down her face and a swell in her throat, Ida Mae tried to sing the next chorus, "None but the righteous, none but the righteous, none but the righteous, shall be saved." She hugged and kissed Little Charles while drying him off. "I'm making all your favorites for dinner."

They all headed back home after church. Little Charles showed off his baptismal certificate to all the neighbors and the new Bible Papa Joe presented to him. Ida Mae finished preparing the dinner she promised Little Charles, assisted by a singing Ivy Lee. Little Charles's favorite meal is fried chicken, buttermilk biscuits, mashed potatoes, and collard greens. He was even happier when Ivy Lee told him she was making him peach cobbler to go with the homemade ice cream for dessert.

As they joined hands and bowed their heads to say grace, Little Charles still grinning from ear to ear and peeking with one eye open, Big Joe with his chest stuck out, all proud of his son, Papa Joe leading the prayer with fervor in his raspy voice, and Willie gently caressing Ivy Lee's hand in his slender calloused one. Ida Mae looked around the table at all her family, each holding a unique piece of her heart reserved for them. She looked forward to a better life in Detroit. She was grateful Papa Joe would fulfill his longstanding promise to his family. Big Joe shuffled between several jobs over the past couple of years, and Willie said he had lost his job at the mill since things were slow.

As Ida Mae turned off the kitchen light, she looked around her old kitchen with its dingy wallpaper and creaking floor. She reminisced about how she stood by Big Mama's side as she taught her how to cook and the many conversations shared with Esterline. Even though she tried, she still could not make her biscuits taste like Big Mama's. Big Joe used to say Big Mama must have held back one secret ingredient. Ida Mae slowly made her way to her bedroom. Her legs ached from the long, busy day of packing.

Ida Mae marked this July day on her calendar months ago. Her pink cotton dress, saturated with sweat, felt like she swam in the St. Johns River on a 90-degree day. She did not know why she bothered to straighten her thick, coarse hair in the muggy, humid Florida heat, but Papa Joe said they should get dressed up for their journey up North. Although spacious, they were packed like sardines into his old, prized sedan, their random belongings in every open crevice. He told them not to worry; "My baby will make it to Uncle Ben's house." Big Joe was in the front seat on the passenger side, next to Little Charles in the middle, and Papa Joe in the driver's seat. In the back were Ida Mae, Ivy Lee, and Willie.

Hattie solemnly stood in the middle of the road until Papa Joe's old sedan was no longer visible. The cloud of dust seemed to dissipate in slow motion. She could not believe Little Charles, her childhood playmate, was gone. She felt so lonely. She and Little Charles were born a week apart, and although they were neighbors, their mothers were best friends and raised them as close as siblings. They spent many days as toddlers and even took their first steps a couple of days apart.

"Hattie, come on in here!" Shouted Esterline. Her voice startled Hattie as she slowly made her way up onto the porch. Esterline held the door open and noticed Hattie trying to hide her face with tears streaming down it. Esterline pulled Hattie in to hug her, not saying a word but letting Hattie sob into her apron. She knew how close the two were and knew it would take time for Hattie to adjust. Esterline was also sad that her best friend, Ida Mae, had left for up North. They grew up together, watched each other's children, and confided in each other. She was more like a sister. She and her husband, Kenneth, both hoped that one day they could move up North, but right now, he was working steadily, and with a baby on the way, it was not the right time.

"Why don't you take and nap? You can help me bake some peanut butter cookies when you wake up."

Hattie nodded and headed to her room in the back of the house.

The emotions washed over Esterline as all the memories flooded in of Ida Mae. She knew Michigan was a long way from Jacksonville, and even with good intentions, she may not see Ida Mae for a long time. They both vowed to write if they could not call and send pictures, even though they knew it would not be the same.

Nausea continued to plague Esterline with this pregnancy. She went through the entire pregnancy with Hattie experiencing no discomfort, and even the birth was easy. *This must be a boy.* She thought as she smiled. She already knew they would name him after her husband if it were a boy, but if it was not, she wanted to name it after her best friend, Ida Mae. Esterline's queasiness calmed down after eating crackers and drinking ginger tea. Although her doctor kept telling her that the morning sickness would subside, it continued. She looked down at the slight protrusion of her stomach and thought about how it would be to start over with a baby. It had been many years since she had a little one around, not for lack of trying. There had been two miscarriages during that time, and then a deep depression followed.

When Papa Joe finally pulled over briefly, Ida Mae convinced everyone to gather for another picture. Papa Joe continued to mill around the car, and Little Charles excitedly posed for the photo. They ate the fried chicken and biscuits she packed, drank their sodas, and ate the lemon pound cake Mrs. Henry, their longtime neighbor, baked for them. Ida Mae thought about how she would miss Mrs. Henry. Mrs. Henry was a close friend to Big Mama and like a mother to Ida Mae after Big Mama died. Ida Mae ensured Little Charles relieved himself in the bushes since there were no gas stations around for Blacks to use. They didn't know when Papa Joe would pull over again.

Big Mama's old brown faded suitcase with the broken lock was tied to the roof. It lay beside two other tattered bags and a chest tightly bound by a thick rope and a weathered black leather one, which Mrs. Henry gave them to spread things out as they struggled to tie them to the car. They squeezed in the minimal luggage Ivy Lee, and Willie brought with them.

The family joined their sweaty palms on the dusty road headed up North, and Papa Joe led a prayer asking God to keep them safe from all hurt, harm, and danger, including the Klan. Little Charles could not stop asking questions about Detroit. Big Joe told him stories from Uncle Ben about the cold weather and the snow. Willie told Little Charles about his summer visit to Ohio when he was ten years old. He told him not to worry about the cold winters; Detroit could get as hot as Jacksonville.

Willie kissed Ivy Lee on her moist cheek. She leaned back and closed her eyes while the humid, dusty breeze caressed her perspiring forehead. Ida Mae put her straw hat back on and got back in the front seat, waiting for sundown, a cool breeze, and road signs to show their exciting journey up North was edging closer. Before Ida Mae knew it, she dozed off and woke to the chirping of crickets and flashing of lightning bugs in the distance. The temperature finally dropped to a more comfortable level.

"We'll git there. You'll see. We will be in Detroit before long. We have to travel through Virginias and Ohio.

"Are we there yet? I want to see my cousin." a groggy Little Charles shifted in the front seat.

"Don't worry, boy, you'll git to see 'em; they are waiting on you. Put your head back down; we'll be there before you knowd it."

Before Papa Joe could barely get the words out, Little Charles was asleep. Ida Mae worried she may not have packed enough food for their trip. This was her first time anywhere outside of Jacksonville. She tried to hold back tears as familiar surroundings had long escaped her view. She tried to hold on to the vision of towering palm trees she knew all her life. Big Joe kept asking her if she was all right, and she nodded her head she was, as he gently patted her on the shoulder. She was a country girl and knew nothing about city life up North.

Papa Joe convinced them it was best for them, and they trusted his judgment. Even though they didn't know Papa Joe's actual age, they knew he was close to eighty. Papa Joe was a vigorous man, but Ida Mae was worried. He kept telling them not to worry about his constant nagging cough. The first time Ida Mae heard his wheezing cough, it scared her. He coughed so hard he got lightheaded, came close to passing out, and stumbled into the yard. Covering his mouth with his old handkerchief and trying to hide what looked like dried blood from Ida Mae. Papa Joe would sit on the back porch and roll tobacco with his swollen, gnarled knuckles stiffened by arthritis and hack from the first puff until he flicked the cigarette into the yard. Still, nothing they said would stop him from smoking.

"You nag me like Big Mama used to. Dats, how I know you are a good woman." He took a drag of his rolled cigarette.

Ivy Lee asked how long before they pulled over as Charles continued to shift in the front seat. Ida Mae could see she was weary, and this trip took its toll on her.

"I'm waiting till I see a good area, Ivy Lee. Can you hold on?"

"Yes, Joe, I'll be all right." Ivy Lee leaned her head back on Willie's shoulder.

The sky was a clear pale blue, and the slight breeze cooled the temperature. It was not as smothering as the steamy Florida air. The sight of a filling station seemed like a mirage in the clearing as they passed endless cornfields.

An old white man with a scraggly gray beard sat on a frayed stool in front of the filling station. He wore a dingy oil-stained undershirt, worn blue jeans held up by loose suspenders, and dusty boots, which made the laces invisible.

"Okay, yawl. I am getting ready to pull over. Don't git out yet. Let me see if we can use this one." Big Joe sighed.

Big Joe put the old dusty car in gear and slowly opened the squeaky driver's door. He was a large man, well over six feet tall and muscular, with a dark chocolate complexion and a sweet disposition. Even though he was the sweetest, kindest man, his size easily intimidated strangers. After closing the rusty door, Big Joe went to the front of the car and scanned the filling station's front and sides for "whites only" signs, seeing none in view.

"Hey there, fella! Yawl lost?" said the old man, standing.

"No sir, we stopped to fill up and use your washroom."

"Okay, it's round back. Beautiful day, ain't it? I'm George. People round here call me Old George."

"Glad to meet you, Mister George.

"Where are yawl headed?"

"We're headed to Detroit," Big Joe responded as he walked up and extended his rough, brawny hand to Old George.

Glad for the business. Don't get much traffic round here. I nodded off and nearly fell off my stool." He gave a hearty laugh and hardly a breath between words. "Is that your family? Tell em to get some air.

Papa Joe was lifting Little Charles from his lap. He had crawled to peer out of the back window several miles before. Papa Joe glared at Big Joe with disappointment. He reminded Big Joe not to be so friendly or too trusting, especially to tell no one where you were going, but Big Joe never listened.

With a nervous scowl, Papa Joe finally made it around the car and closer to where Big Joe was standing. Old George introduced himself to Papa Joe and extended his hand. Papa Joe obliged with a brief handshake and hurried back to the car to open the door for Ida Mae. The long ride made him stiffen.

Old George offered them cold sodas at no charge after Little Charles talked with him about how excited he was to go to Detroit. Little Charles was friendly, like Big Joe. Ida Mae kept reminding him to go to the bathroom after all the soda he had consumed. Her jaw dropped as she looked over at Little Charles standing bare feet in the dusty road.

Ida Mae pulled the picnic basket and blanket from the trunk. She asked Old George if it was alright if they sat at a weather-worn wooden table propped up against the side of the building. He obliged. Big Joe turned it over, and Ida Mae covered it with the blanket. Ida Mae passed out the leftovers. After praying over the food, Papa Joe sat in the driver's seat to eat his meal. There was enough to share with Old George; he was so grateful and said it was years since he had eaten a good meal like this one. There was nothing left of Mrs. Henry's lemon pound cake but crumbs. *Ida Mae thought I should have kept it in the front seat instead of in the back with Big Joe and Little Charles.*

After everyone rested and Ida Mae suggested they tend to their needs, they said their goodbyes to Old George. They joined hands by the car to say another prayer before they got back on the route. Before Papa Joe began, Old George limped over to their circle and joined hands with Big Joe and Little Charles, which surprised all of them.

Papa Joe began. "Father God, cover and protect this family as we travel this road. Keep us safe from hurt, harm, and danger as we make our way. Amen."

Dusk was settling in as they reentered the car. Big Joe insisted on taking the wheel and headed down the road. Ida Mae could see Old George standing on the sandy road, sadly waving goodbye. He wished them well and warned them to be cautious. Even though they were on a bumpy dirt road, the scenery was beautiful, and the sweet scent of magnolia trees filled the air.

Little Charles perked up after their last stop, and he and Ida Mae chatted about what it might be like in Detroit. When he began squirming around in the front seat, she suspected he drank too many sodas back at the gas station generously offered by Old George, and they would have to stop again soon.

"Okay, Charles, I know you have to go. We are pulling over. Don't go too far. Your daddy will watch out for you," said Ida Mae. After a few minutes, Little Charles came running excitedly towards the car.

"Come on, Little Charles, get back in. Let's get going," said Big Joe.

"Daddy, I saw a parade across a field. Everybody was in costumes like Halloween. They were white, and the hats were pointy, like witches' hats. Did you see them?"

"What? Where? What did you see?" Papa Joe grabbed Little Charles firmly by the shoulders.

"They looked like ghosts by the big tree over there!" said Little Charles, pointing.

"Dats da Klan, boy! You think they saw you?" Papa Joe's head perspired, and his eyes widened.

"No, Papa Joe, I bent down in the grass. They were looking up at a tree." Little Charles appeared frightened and thought he had done something wrong.

"You all right, boy, you ain't in trouble, but it's time tuh git." Papa Joe rushed Little Charles into the front seat.

Papa Joe and Big Joe exchanged uneasy glances and quickly got back on the road. They were all silent until they were halfway to the Ohio state line. No one got any sleep, not even Little Charles. Big Joe kept on driving. Even Big Joe seemed jolted by their close encounter, and nothing shook him.

As they turned onto Log Cabin Street on the northwest side of Detroit and parked in front of Uncle Ben's house, Ida Mae noticed the fresh scent of lilacs. The tree-lined street was paved and wide. The family would have to get used to no dirt roads or palm trees. Ida Mae longed for Jacksonville but pushed the feeling away and focused on their new surroundings.

"Yawl finally made it!" shrieked Aunt Lillian. "We have been praying for yawl." Aunt Lillian was waiting on the porch for them, wearing a brightly colored red apron with daisies covering her wide hips with her hand on each side. "Come get out of the hot car. We got a big dinner fixed for yawl." Her thick, wavy silver hair pulled back in a tight bun. She was a big-boned, light-skinned woman with freckles sprinkled across her nose. She reminded Ida Mae of their old neighbor, Mrs. Henry. Little Charles ran up the porch and hugged Aunt Lillian. Two of Aunt Lillian's God children, Daniel and Loretta, were peeking out the screen door. Daniel was about Little Charles' age, and Loretta was a couple of years older than Little Charles. The two of them were excited.

"Come on, Brother, I've been waiting to hug your neck for such a long time," Uncle Ben shuffled out of the side gate with tears in his eyes. "You look like Daddy with less hair." Papa Joe laughed, too.

Papa Joe, teary-eyed, slowly hobbled around the car. It was clear the ride stiffened his limbs. They embraced each other in a long hug and patted each other's backs as they pulled out handkerchiefs and wiped away tears.

Ida Mae felt a lump in her throat as she witnessed their touching exchange. They were the last two children left. Four sisters and three brothers passed before them. The siblings dreamed of coming up North but were the only two who accomplished it.

Ida Mae looked up as Big Joe came to help her out of the car while Willie was helping Ivy Lee out of the back seat.

Uncle Ben and Aunt Lillian's home was small and neat, and Ida Mae wondered how they would put all of them up. They kept reassuring them there was plenty of room. Ivy Lee and Willie would stay with Mabel, Ivy Lee's Sister, who owned the two-family flat across the street.

"Ida Mae, you ain't aged a bit. Come here and give me a big hug." Aunt Lillian held her arms out.

"I'm so glad we made it like Papa Joe said we would. Thank you so very much for putting us up. We sure appreciate it," Ida Mae responded.

"Yawl is family, and it is what families do."

Big Joe entered last after holding the door for the rest of them to join. Ida Mae could smell the aroma of a down-home dinner from the kitchen. Lillian was an excellent cook, and Ida Mae knew a feast awaited.

"She has been cooking for days, waiting for Yawl's arrival." Beamed Uncle Ben.

They took turns in the bathroom, freshening up from the long trip. Each member went to the dining room, the largest room in the tiny house. Aunt Lillian's buffet was covered with food, with more dishes in the kitchen. She set up a small wooden card table for the kids. A beautiful beige lace tablecloth covered her sizable dining room table, which matched the drapes. The bottom of the fancy wooden table revealed mahogany table legs shaped like enormous paws. Ida Mae imagined kids hiding under the big table. In front of each of the seven chairs was a beautiful setting with white dinner plates, sterling silver flatware, and fancy crystal-stemmed glasses.

Little Charles was in the corner giggling with Daniel and Loretta, who he had already dubbed as his cousins. Ida Mae's eyes widened as she took in the sight of this spread. Aunt Lillian arranged on the buffet a tossed salad, black-eyed peas, creamed corn, chitterlings, fried chicken, mashed potatoes, candied yams, macaroni and cheese, collard and turnip greens, cornbread, fluffy brown dinner rolls, and for dessert, a giant chocolate cake, two sweet potato pies, and a pound cake as appetizing as Mrs. Henry's. In the center of the table was a white gravy boat trimmed in tiny pink flowers, matching the dinner plates filled to the brim with creamy brown gravy. Surrounding the freshly cut sunflowers in the glass vase in the center of the table were two large pitchers, one with lemonade and one with sun tea, both garnished with freshly sliced lemons. Ida Mae overlooked the most inviting ham covered in a glistening brown sugar glaze and juicy pineapples.

They all joined hands as Uncle Ben prayed over the food and thanked God for his family and their safe arrival in Detroit. Ida Mae sat between Papa Joe and her Big Joe as she looked around and saw how blessed they were to be there with family.

Papa Joe looked over at Ida Mae and nodded. "I told you we would make it, Ida Mae."

She leaned over and gave Papa Joe a kiss on his bristly cheek. "I didn't have any doubt. Thank you."

They all began passing around the many dishes Aunt Lillian had prepared, and it was not too long before they were all full and satisfied by the vast, delicious meal. They talked about their journey and the meeting with Old George. Papa Joe told Uncle Ben about the Klan they saw while traveling and how swiftly they made their way out of that area. Uncle Ben said he was worried they might travel through parts of the Midwest where he heard the Klan remained strong and sundown towns still existed. He understood some of the same gruesome things he and his brother Ben and their Father and uncles experienced in the deep south were still common. Papa Joe never forgot the image of his cousin Latham hanging from a tree and the group of people cheering as his soiled, bloodied body swung back and forth in the middle of an obscured field.

Ivy Lee and Ida Mae helped Aunt Lillian clear the table and clean the kitchen. At the same time, Loretta and Daniel led Little Charles to the massive backyard. Ida Mae found Little Charles' shoes under the table, and she shook her head. Papa Joe and Uncle Ben sat on the front porch reminiscing while Big Joe and Willie unloaded their belongings from the car. It was a long day, and Ida Mae could not wait to lay her head on a soft pillow and cool sheets.

They settled Ivy Lee and Willie across the street at Mabel's home. They tucked the rest into every corner of Aunt Lillian and Uncle Ben's tiny bungalow. Many years had passed since Ivy Lee and Mabel saw each other, and according to Aunt Lillian, Uncle Ben's wife, Mabel was domineering, and the relationship was strained.

The kids retired to a back room on pallets Aunt Lillian had laid out. Ida Mae could still hear them whispering and giggling in the background while Aunt Lillian tried to hush them. Papa Joe stayed in a bedroom in the basement, and Ida Mae could hear his hacking cough through the creaky floorboards. Ida Mae and Big Joe nestled in the extra room on the first floor. She cuddled up close to him while looking out of the moonlit window, realizing she was many miles away from Jacksonville's palm trees and damp heat. It was bittersweet. She could not have been happier. She drifted off to sleep, eager to start their new life in Michigan.

After a month passed, Big Joe started a new job at Ford Motor Company on the assembly line, and Ivy Lee and Willie settled across the street at Mabel's house in the upstairs flat. Little Charles and Riley, Mabel's son, were daily playmates. Aunt Lillian enjoyed Ida Mae joining her in the kitchen and watching soap operas together. Papa Joe and Uncle Ben spent hours talking about their childhood. The garage was their favorite spot to sit.

One morning, Ida Mae noticed Papa Joe moving a little slower than usual, and he went to lie back down after breakfast, which was unusual for him. She told him she would check on him, even though he assured her he was fine. Later, he went to sit on the screened-in porch in the adjacent rocking chair alongside Uncle Ben. Their raucous laughter flowed throughout the house. Suddenly, Papa Joe began coughing, which was not unusual, but this time, it seemed like he could not stop or catch his breath.

Ida Mae rushed to get him a glass of water, heading back towards the front door. She heard Uncle Ben yell, "Call the ambulance!" Ida Mae dropped the glass of water she was carrying. It crashed to the floor short of the front door. As she ran onto the porch, she noticed Papa Joe slumped over in the chair.

"Papa Joe! Papa Joe!" she screamed.

"Brother! Brother!" Uncle Ben tried to rouse Papa Joe.

Aunt Lillian appeared in the doorway. "The ambulance is on the way!"

Papa Joe wasn't breathing, and his eyes rolled back in his head. His skin was pale and ashen, and his thin lips turned blue.

A short time later, the ambulance attendants filed in quickly. Each of them focused on a specific task. Uncle Ben leaned on his wooden cane as he stood on the front lawn, looking up nervously at the screened-in porch. All he could see was one attendant's bobbing up and down as he did multiple chest compressions on Papa Joe. Aunt Lillian stayed inside the front door as Ida Mae watched in horror from the dusty corner of the porch, holding her breath, horrified at what she was witnessing. Ida Mae wished Big Joe were there, but it would be a few hours before he came home, and there was no way to reach him at the factory.

Ida Mae sat in the rocking chair where Papa Joe had sat a short time ago, wringing her hands, waiting for Big Joe to be dropped off by his friend. *How would she tell Big Joe and Little Charles that Papa Joe was gone?* Ida Mae thought. She asked Mabel to keep Little Charles across the street until Big Joe arrived. Fortunately, Little Charles and Riley were playing in the basement. They were not aware of the sirens or flashing lights of the ambulance.

Aunt Lillian arranged for a funeral home owned by one of her church members to pick up Papa Joe's body from the morgue. Ida Mae wished they could have waited for Big Joe, but she later found out he worked overtime.

Aunt Lillian and Uncle Ben sheltered in their bedroom. Ida Mae could hear their muffled sobs coming from an open window.

"My Brother, he just got here, nooooo!"

Ida Mae tried to pull herself together for Big Joe and Little Charles. Little Charles was a baby when Big Mama died, so this would be his first time experiencing a death. Little Charles adored Papa Joe even though Papa Joe could be a little abrasive; it was the way Papa Joe showed love.

Hours passed as Ida Mae continued rocking on the front porch. She felt dazed, sullen, and stunned. As the sun went down, she heard Big Joe's friend Lawrence's noisy truck approaching. The brakes were equally loud, making a rusty screeching sound. Big Joe got out laughing as he slammed the heavily corroded door and headed up the short, paved walkway.

"Hey, Sweetie!" He pulled the aluminum door to the screened-in porch. Ida Mae paced over to Big Joe, quickly squeezing him in a tight embrace as she pulled back and touched her hand to his stubbly unshaven chin while looking deep into his eyes from her tear-filled ones. "He's gone. Papa Joe is gone."

Big Joe's expression let her know he understood every word she said. He held her tight as she squeezed his muscular frame and felt him shudder, shake, and tremble as he started weeping. Big Joe fell into Uncle Ben's rocking chair, covering his face with his large hands.

After he settled down and she explained what had happened, he asked about Little Charles. When Ida Mae told him Little Charles didn't know, he said he would deliver the sad news. As Big Joe and Ida Mae entered the house, Uncle Ben and Aunt Lillian exited the back bedroom, holding hands.

Uncle Ben walked straight over and hugged his nephew. "Brother is gone, but I thank God he let us be together one last time. Come on, yawl, let us pray." He stretched out his arms, embracing the small group. "Father God, the

God of Abraham, Isaac, and Jacob, we love you and know you make no mistakes. Send the comforter to this family. We find comfort in knowing he is in your loving arms and will commune with those loved ones gone before him. Give Big Joe the strength to comfort his son and let him know there is everlasting life. Father, thank you for my brother and the years we spent together. I ask for strength in your mighty and precious name, Jesus. Amen."

They all embraced, and Big Joe headed out the door in a slow shuffle across the street to get Little Charles. Ida Mae alerted Mabel he was on his way.

*P*apa *Joe is gone*, Ida Mae thought to herself. He was the only real father figure since she never knew her Father. He embraced her as a daughter when she and Big Joe began dating, telling her she was perfect for Big Joe. *How do I say goodbye?* She wondered.

Aunt Lillian busied herself in the kitchen, preparing a casserole with a few ingredients instead of the elaborate meals she usually prepared. Dinner was subdued. Little Charles picked at his dinner and asked to go back across the street to play with Riley.

Big Joe, Uncle Ben, Aunt Lillian, and Ida Mae met Deacon Wallace at the funeral home the following day. Uncle Ben laid $600 on the desk, paying for the funeral. "I want to send my brother home, right."

Ida Mae's stomach was uneasy with every step they took toward the casket room. She squeezed Big Joe's hand, and he patted her hand to reassure her.

They agreed on a dark gray metal casket with a pale gray interior. Papa Joe loved flowers, so they selected a beautiful spray of white roses to adorn his casket.

"I want a lively homegoing to celebrate my dear brother's life."

"I will ask Ivy Lee to sing at the funeral." Ida Mae volunteered eagerly.

"In case Little Charles wants to say something, please leave room in the program." Big Joe added. Deacon Wallace assured them everything would flow smoothly.

As they left the funeral home and headed towards the car, Aunt Lillian whispered to Ida Mae. "Are you sure you want Ivy Lee involved? Mabel says that she can be unpredictable. Run it by her, but consider the source. I think Mabel exaggerates."

"During the time I have spent with Ivy Lee while she was staying with us, she seemed to be fine, although she seemed a little agitated during the ride here; I think we all felt that way. It was such a long ride. She was sweet and helpful to me. I will speak to Mabel, but it will be fine. Papa Joe heard her sing at Little Charles' baptism and loved it."

Big Joe pulled out Papa Joe's black suit when they returned home. It was one he wore on certain occasions and consistently every Sunday. He kept it on a hanger with a newly starched white shirt and striped tie. This was Big Joe's first time realizing or thinking the deceased needed underwear and socks. Uncle Ben wanted to buy a new suit for Papa Joe, but Big Joe and Ida Mae talked him out of it. Papa Joe was frugal and would not want any money squandered, especially on him.

Ida Mae contacted Mabel about Ivy Lee singing at Papa Joe's funeral the following day. She initially had no reservations but kept thinking about what Aunt Lillian had said.

"Good morning, Mabel. It's Ida Mae. May I come by?"

"Yes, of course. Have you eaten breakfast yet?"

"No, I haven't."

"Well, give me about a half hour, and I will have things ready."

"Okay, see you then."

Ida Mae inhaled the crisp summer air wafting through the window as the curtains blew. The sun shone through Aunt Lillian's living room sheers, brightening a dismal morning. She dressed and headed across the street as everyone was waking up, and Aunt Lillian wished her luck. The summer Michigan weather was a refreshing change from

49

Jacksonville's muggy, stifling heat this time of year. Ida Mae experienced being homesick, but missing the humidity was not one of them. All the Detroit family warned her she would feel different when winter arrived. Ida Mae, who has never seen snow before, is excited. As she approached the door, she noticed Ivy Lee standing in the doorway with a big smile.

"Good morning, Ida Mae. I've been praying for all of you."

"Good morning! Thank you so much. We appreciate your prayers."

"How are you?" Ivy Lee said in a concerned tone. I am so sorry to hear about Papa Joe. He made it all the way here." She opened the door and reached out, giving Ida Mae a warm embrace and kissing her on the cheek.

"I'm holding up. Papa Joe was determined to get us here." A lump formed in her throat.

"Ivy Lee, is that Ida Mae?"

"Yes, it is," responded Ivy Lee.

Ivy Lee led Ida Mae to the dining room. The large table dwarfed the place setting for two.

"Sit down, please, Ida Mae. Make yourself at home."

Ivy Lee patted Ida Mae on the shoulder as she headed back towards the stairs leading to the upper flat where she and Willie lived.

"Oh, Mabel! You shouldn't have gone to all this trouble." Ida Mae looked over the place setting and the table set before her.

"It's no trouble."

Ida Mae prayed, and they ate fresh strawberries, blueberries, crispy bacon, scrambled eggs, fluffy homemade biscuits, and drank piping hot coffee and freshly squeezed orange juice.

Ida Mae's dress tightened around her full stomach after partaking in the delicious meal, and she offered to clear the dishes, but Mabel would not hear of it.

"No, honey! You are my guest; I will get to those later. Let's go into the living room."

They sat on the large green sofa decorated with gold buttons in its overstuffed arms. Ida Mae exhaled, and Mabel could sense how difficult it was for her to speak about Papa Joe. Mabel immediately embraced Ida Mae, as she could see her blinking as tears welled in her eyes and ran down her cheeks.

"Thank you, Mabel." She tried to catch her breath between sobs. "I have been trying to be strong for Big Joe and Little Charles." She took the white handkerchief with tiny daisies on its border being offered by Mabel.

"You needed to let it out, honey. Papa Joe was like a father to you. Can't be close without feeling some pain. Keep those memories close, and they will make you smile. You will get through this."

"Well, we planned the funeral yesterday. The funeral will be on Saturday at 11:00 a.m. at Uncle Ben's church, Foothill Missionary Baptist Church, where he's a Deacon. One deacon at his church owns the small funeral home that will oversee the service. I wanted to ask whether you think Ivy Lee would be up to singing at his funeral. Papa Joe enjoyed hearing her sing."

Mabel exhaled while taking Ida Mae's hand in hers. "Well..." Mabel leaned in closer to Ida Mae and lowered her voice. Suddenly Ivy Lee appeared in the doorway between the kitchen and the dining room with a clear view of where Ida Mae and Mabel were sitting. "I would love to sing at Papa Joe's funeral! It would be an honor." Mabel, clearly agitated with a scowl, stood up and turned in Ivy Lee's direction. "Ivy Lee, you should not be listening to our conversation!"

"I'm sorry, sister. Taking care of the dishes for you, and I overheard you talking. Didn't mean to interrupt."

"Are you sure you're up to it? Mabel said as she walked over and whispered to Ivy Lee. You have not been feeling your best lately, you know. You've been feeling down and in bed the last two days. Willie is worried about you."

"I feel fine, sister. I feel fine!"

"Okay, Ivy Lee, okay!" Mabel quickly silenced an enthusiastic Ivy Lee. She returned to the couch next to Ida Mae. Her tight lips held an angry scowl. She lowered her head, put one hand on her forehead, and inhaled to compose herself before speaking. Ida Mae fidgeted in the seat, looking back at Ivy Lee and then at Mabel. She felt awkward in the middle of this conversation. It wasn't clear to her what was happening between the two sisters. She wondered if it was a mistake to have made this request of Ivy Lee. Aunt Lillian warned her, but Ida Mae's interactions with Ivy Lee were pleasant.

"Ivy Lee, maybe *Blessed Assurance* or *Precious Lord?* Those were Papa Joe's favorites."

"I can sing them both. Thank you for asking me, cousin." Ivy Lee reached over and hugged Ida Mae and then walked into the kitchen to resume washing dishes.

"Let's go get some fresh air." Mabel took Ida Mae by the arm and led her to the front door.

"Mabel, I hope I didn't do anything wrong?"

"No, no, it's Ivy Lee. She can be unpredictable."

"What do you mean? She was wonderful during the time we spent together in Jacksonville."

"Her mind, baby, it sometimes ain't right. No spells in a while, and she loves singing, so I can only hope it will be fine."

Ida Mae's eyes widened. "Should I?"

"No, I saw her eyes light up. It has been a while since I've seen that. She has down days, and the next thing you know, she will clean the house from the ceiling to the basement. I don't understand it. One minute she will be fine, and then her mood changes. Willie wants her to go to the doctor. He is wonderful with her. This may be good for her. Write the arrangements down, and I'll let Willie know."

"Okay, I'll write it down and have Little Charles return it. Thank you so much for breakfast and everything."

They chatted a short while longer and then embraced again before a perplexed Ida Mae made her way across the street.

Aunt Lillian was waiting for her in the doorway as she opened the door. "So, how did it go?"

"Everything went fine. I broke down and didn't even realize I held that in. Mabel was comforting." Ida Mae needed help understanding the history between Mabel and Lillian. Although curious, she did not want to ask.

"Mabel, comforting?" Aunt Lillian's face looked doubtful.

"Yes, she was sweet. Also, Ivy Lee agreed to sing two songs: *Blessed Assurance* and *Precious Lord.* I will write the arrangements and send it by Little Charles."

"Well, I'm surprised but glad everything went well." Aunt Lillian said with her hand on her hip.

"Come here, chile!" she hugged Ida Mae.

Ida Mae watched Little Charles skip back across the paved street after he paused, looking for traffic in both directions.

The sunrise on this cool summer morning revealed streaks of sunrays peeking around the edges of the living room shades. Aunt Lillian's house was quiet, but Ida Mae could not sleep as usual. Between Big Joe's snoring and Ida Mae's insomnia, she seemed to be the first one awake. Ida Mae prayed the funeral service would proceed in a way to honor Papa Joe's memory. *The sun is shining for Papa Joe*, she thought. Oh, how he loved a clear summer day to fish in the St. John's River.

All the family, Aunt Lillian, Uncle Ben, Big Joe, Ida Mae, and Little Charles, each arrived to sit in the immaculate living room. Little Charles was quiet but fidgeting. One by one, they all stood quietly, realizing that the person they were waiting to lead them in prayer was gone to be with the ancestors.

Simultaneously they joined hands, and Uncle Ben, though teary-eyed, led them in prayer and ended as Deacon Wallace knocked on the door to alert them of the family car's arrival.

Ida Mae could not help but think back to their journey up north and Papa Joe repeating, "We'll git there." *He was right, we all made it, and I believe he is resting in peace after safely delivering us to Detroit, despite his old sedan,* she thought.

The pews were filled with church members. Uncle Ben and Aunt Lillian were the first ones to line up. Little Charles wedged between Ida Mae and Big Joe, gripping his mother's hand as he looked down at the worn red carpet that lined the narrow center aisle.

They lay Papa Joe in a dark gray casket in the suit he wore on special occasions with a freshly starched white shirt. He appeared at peace. *Ida Mae thought if anyone was in heaven, it was Papa Joe.*

They each stopped briefly at the casket. Ida Mae planted a kiss on Papa Joe's cold, stiff forehead. Little Charles' eyes filled with tears as he took his seat. After the family was all seated, the other attendees greeted each mourning family member sitting in the first pew.

Ida Mae noticed Cousin Willie walking Ivy Lee up to the pulpit, holding her by the arm while helping her up the stairs to the choir stand area. Ida Mae felt Mabel nervously shifting, seated next to her. About six choir members assembled in their royal blue choir robes trimmed in gold to render *Bye and Bye* and *When We All Get to Heaven*; the two upbeat songs Uncle Ben requested,

Ivy Lee wore a beautiful pale pink flowy dress with a matching hat. She looked serene; her full lips glistened with bright red lipstick, and with a slight grin on her face. Ivy Lee approached the microphone opposite the central podium and took a deep breath at the introduction of the music. She looked radiant and confident in her first solo. The organist gave her a nod, and the biggest smile came across her heart-shaped face. Her gold front tooth shone like a diamond. She captivated the audience from the moment she parted her lips.

Reverend Hurd opened with a prayer and introduced Ivy Lee to sing what would be the most beautiful rendition of *Blessed Assurance* Ida Mae had ever heard. Ida Mae thought how much Papa Joe would have loved it. She glimpsed at a relieved Mabel sitting to her left.

Aunt Lillian read the obituary, followed by remarks. Although hesitant, Ida Mae headed to the podium after the obituary reading. She could not sit there without conveying her feelings about Papa Joe. Ida Mae found speaking challenging, but she swallowed hard and spoke.

"When Big Joe introduced me to Papa Joe, he treated me like a daughter. He told me I nagged him just like Big Joe's mother. I am really going to miss him. He promised us we would make it to Detroit, and we did. I'm so sad he didn't have more time." Her voice trailed off. As she was about to finish, Little Charles stood beside her and whispered he wanted to speak.

"Papa Joe showed me how to polish my shoes on our back porch. I made them shine just like he told me." He looked down at his shoes. "I miss him." He dashed back to his seat and scooted up close to Big Joe.

Reverend Hurd approached the pulpit, his massive frame filling out his flowing black robe trimmed in gold. He adjusted the microphone to deliver the brief eulogy and wiped his perspiring forehead with his large white handkerchief.

"I met Joseph Connor, or Papa Joe as you know him, just a few months ago. His bellowing voice echoed through the church. "Mr. Connor reminded me of my grandfather: strong, proud, and God-fearing. He shared many stories with me, but what was clear was his love for his family. He was so happy to be in Detroit and united with his brother, Ben. His many years of service in the church was his glory, and he quoted his favorite scripture, *Proverbs 3:5-6 Trust in the Lord with all thine heart; and lean not unto thine own understanding. In all thy ways acknowledge him, and he shall direct thy paths.*" That is something we had in common. That is my favorite scripture as well. I was happy to welcome him to our Deacon board as I'm sure the other deacons would agree." Reverend Hurd looked towards a teary-eyed Uncle Ben. His hands tightly clasped with Aunt Lillian's. "Thank you for sharing your brother with us. He was a blessing, and the love you two shared was clear. May the memories that you shared comfort you. He went to be with his ancestors." Reverend Hurd looked down at Papa Joe's open casket while closing his Bible. "Well done, good and faithful servant."

It was time for one last solo by Ivy Lee. She took her place at the microphone and sang *Take My Hand, Precious Lord.* The church did not have a dry eye when she sang the final note, including Ivy Lee. The church nurses hurriedly passed out tissue to the packed church.

The casket remained open during the ceremony. Ida Mae dreaded this time when the funeral directors asked if anyone wanted to come forward for final viewing. Big Joe, quiet throughout the service, approached the casket with Uncle Ben. Big Joe began sobbing uncontrollably as Uncle Ben tried to console him. They slowly took their seats as the coffin was closed, and several church ladies carried flowers to the hearse. Big Joe composed himself enough to take his place beside Willie and the other deacons to serve as pallbearers. The family followed their patriarch's casket in a solemn procession out of the church.

The cemetery was a short drive away. When the family arrived, six chairs were set up by the graveside underneath the green tent: one for Ida Mae, Uncle Ben, Aunt Lillian, Big Joe, and Little Charles. Little Charles motioned for Ivy Lee to sit beside him, which she obliged.

As Reverend Hurd placed the carnations over the casket as a cross and said the last words committing his body to the ground, Ivy Lee sang *Amazing Grace.* It was beautiful and seemed to comfort everyone.

Big Joe was the last to leave the graveside. Ida Mae tried to comfort him as he broke down again as they lowered the casket into the earth.

The family retreated to the waiting family car. They were all quiet for the ride back to the church, where a repast prepared by the Deaconess awaited them.

Before Ida Mae sat down to eat, she approached Ivy Lee and hugged her.

"Ivy Lee, Thank you so much. It was beautiful. Papa Joe would have loved both songs. He enjoyed your lovely voice."

"Thank you for allowing me to sing at his home going. It was my honor." Ida Mae took her seat between Big Joe and Mabel. Ivy Lee sat at the corner of the table next to Willie. Reverend Hurd blessed the food, and they dined on a beautiful meal.

Mabel turned to Ida Mae with a relieved look on her face. "I'm so glad everything went well. I overreacted, and I apologize."

"No need to apologize. I appreciate your support. I'm so glad Ivy Lee could sing. Papa Joe loved her voice. We had a service Papa Joe would have been proud of.

Big Joe was settling into his job at the factory, and they all seemed to adjust to the void left in their lives by the absence of Papa Joe. Big Joe and Ida Mae focused on saving enough money to move to a place of their own and a possible visit from Esterline. They had been looking at a small city surrounded by Detroit called Highland Park, touted for its excellent school system.